The Night Thief

The Night Thief

BARBARA FRADKIN

RAVEN BOOKS
an imprint of
ORCA BOOK PUBLISHERS

Library and Archives Canada Cataloguing in Publication

Fradkin, Barbara Fraser, 1947–, author
The night thief / Barbara Fradkin.
(Rapid Reads)

Issued also in print and electronic formats.
ISBN 978-1-4598-0866-9 (pbk.).—ISBN 978-1-4598-0867-6 (pdf).—
ISBN 978-1-4598-0868-3 (epub)

I. Title. II. Series: Rapid reads
PS8561.R233N54 2015   C813'.6   C2014-906675-9
C2014-906676-7

First published in the United States, 2015
Library of Congress Control Number: 2014952061

Summary: Cedric O'Toole, an unlikely sleuth, sets out to discover
who has been stealing from his farm. (RL 3.2)

MIX
Paper from
responsible sources
FSC® C103214
www.fsc.org

*Orca Book Publishers is dedicated to preserving the environment and has
printed this book on Forest Stewardship Council® certified paper.*

Orca Book Publishers gratefully acknowledges the support for
its publishing programs provided by the following agencies:
the Government of Canada through the Canada Book Fund and the
Canada Council for the Arts, and the Province of British Columbia
through the BC Arts Council and the Book Publishing Tax Credit.

Cover design by Jenn Playford
Cover photography by Getty Images

ORCA BOOK PUBLISHERS
PO Box 5626, Stn. B
Victoria, BC Canada
V8R 6S4

ORCA BOOK PUBLISHERS
PO Box 468
Custer, WA USA
98240-0468

www.orcabook.com
Printed and bound in Canada.

18 17 16 15 • 4 3 2 1

*This book is dedicated to all the teachers,
social workers and community workers
who hold the welfare and happiness of
children close to their hearts.*

One

It was supposed to be a perfect October night. The moon was huge and the sky so clear I could see all the way across the field to the woods.

But after less than an hour, I was freezing to death. My toes had gone numb. My back ached and I couldn't feel the tip of my nose. Good move, O'Toole, I grumbled to myself as I eased my stiff fingers from the shotgun. You couldn't wear a warmer jacket?

I was lying in wait for the night thief. For more than three weeks now, I'd been trying to stop him from raiding my vegetable patch. My usual scarecrows and whirligigs had been useless. So first I'd welded together a tall fence using every piece of metal I could spare. Bits of car hoods and washing machines, rusty pipes and chicken wire. It wasn't pretty, but I thought it would do the trick.

It didn't. The next night he dug up a whole row of baby carrots and snapped a prize ear of Peaches and Cream corn off its stalk. So I put chicken wire over the whole garden. A foot-long zucchini disappeared. I'd never seen anything like it. I share this backcountry piece of scrub my mother called a farm with lots of wildlife. I don't mind a rabbit stealing a carrot or two, or a deer nibbling the buds off my flowers. But this beast, whatever it was, had to be feeding a whole village!

I don't ask for much. I know the locals laugh at my organic garden, my milk goat and my fields of rusted junk. But I like to invent things. You never know when that three-wheeled ATV might make me a million dollars. In the meantime, I get by with handyman jobs and my vegetables, which my aunt Penny sells at her corner grocery store in the village. This night thief was seriously messing with my livelihood.

So next I got out my welding torch again and surrounded the whole garden with homemade humane traps. I caught a groundhog and a skunk, but the rest of the bait, along with half a dozen more ears of corn, was gone.

My dog was no help either. Chevy is a border collie mix who barks if a leaf blows across the yard. Usually she sleeps on my bed, but for three nights I tied her out by the vegetable patch. I figured her barking would chase off anything. The first night she did bark, but by the time I ran downstairs and out to the back field, she was wagging her tail and there was nothing in sight.

After that she didn't even bark. Even when my best crop of cherry tomatoes went missing. A chill ran through me. What *was* this thing? What kind of creature could get through my fence, steal the bait from my traps and hypnotize my dog?

That's when I oiled up my mother's shotgun. I hate guns. Hate the sight of blood, to tell the truth, ever since I was nineteen and had to identify my mother's body in what was left of her car. But now I wasn't just angry. I was spooked.

I didn't plan to kill it. I can't shoot a tin can off a stump at three feet. But I did plan to scare it off into someone else's vegetable patch. Now, as I crouched behind the shed with my fingers growing numb, I wondered if it had outsmarted me again.

Just half an hour longer, I told myself. The dry cornstalks stood like stiff sentries in the moonlight. An owl hooted. A coyote yipped. Then a dark shape came out of the trees. Hunched and formless, it floated across the field. I stared at it, hardly daring to breathe. A bear cub?

Behind me a twig cracked, and I gasped. Spun around, waving my gun. Nothing. I turned back just in time to see the dark shape melt back into the woods.

Damn!

I waited until the moon slid low in the sky and the shadows grew long. But the creature never came back. The next night I wore my parka and hid behind a tall stand of goldenrod near the woods. The wind was up, blowing clouds across the moon. The grass rippled and danced, making it hard to see. As I waited, my mind drifted. A hairy werewolf was sneaking across my land, slipping the latch on my back door and coming up my stairs...

I awoke with a jolt. Sat up to see a black creature moving through my garden, bending, reaching, scooping. I almost shouted aloud. Hunched low in the grass, I raced closer. Its shape was half hidden by the corn. Too skinny for a bear but too big for a raccoon. I watched as it unwound the wire at the corner of my fence, slipped out through the hole and turned back to reattach the fence.

What the hell?

I ducked lower as the creature, cradling its armload of loot, scurried past and headed back toward the trees. I kept fifty feet between us as I followed it. In the forest, even the weak moonlight disappeared. The figure became a shadow that moved quickly in and out of the trees. It was like it could see in the dark. I couldn't. I tripped over roots and cracked my head on branches. Before long, the shadow was gone.

The next day after work, I put Chevy on a leash and set off into the forest. Everything I know about tracking comes from watching bad Westerns on TV. But Chevy knows even less. So I was surprised when she began to wag her tail and pulled ahead in the direction the night thief had taken. Fallen leaves swished under our feet, making so much noise I figured any creature from here to the county line would be long gone.

Chevy led me deep into the forest. This was all part of my back woodlot, an untamed jungle of boulders and fallen trees. As a kid I had loved to play here, bored by my mother's endless Elvis records and TV soap operas. Imagining I was Robin Hood, I had built a cave in the roots of an old maple that hung over a cliff. Chevy headed straight there. As we got closer, I saw the ground in front was trampled. A pine bough blocked the entrance to the cave.

I froze. Terrified of what lurked inside the cave. Wishing I had brought my gun.

But Chevy knocked aside the branch and barged straight in, her tail wagging. Inside, she raced around snuffling the ground. I crouched in the middle, bewildered. The cave was empty, but the dirt floor was covered by an old horse blanket from my barn.

Outside, I searched for clues. There was a circle of ashes in the clearing and an old microwave full of my vegetables down by the stream. Astonishment shot through me.

"Wow, old girl!" I said. "We have squatters. Can you figure out where they've run off to?"

I led her in a big circle around the camp, hoping she'd pick up the trail. She doubled back and forth, confused. That's when all those years of watching Westerns with my mother came in handy. Chevy's not a fan of water, so I had to drag her across the stream. But sure enough, on the other side she took off with her nose to the ground and her tail in the air. My night thief must have watched the same Westerns. How to lose the sheriff on your tail.

Forests change all the time. Trees fall, others grow, shadows deepen. But I'd fought many make-believe battles in these woods, and I knew every bluff and rock. I jogged as fast as Chevy could pull me. The afternoon sun was sinking fast. It was almost gone before I caught my first glimpse of movement ahead. A flash of gray against the red leaves. Maybe a deer or a coyote. But maybe not. I picked up my pace. I'm not a big guy, but luckily I'd been hauling cement bags on a construction site all summer. Between that and my gardening, I'd packed on some muscle. I was breathing hard, but I was gaining. Another flash of gray, scrambling up the hillside.

I let Chevy go and she raced ahead, her tail wagging. She bounced in circles around the figure as it tried to run.

"Stop!" I shouted. "I won't hurt you!"

The figure dived into the bushes. I ran forward, rounded the bush and nearly fell over a small boy huddled behind a rock. Chevy was licking his face.

The kid looked like he'd been dragged out of a coal bin. His hair was one long tangle, and he nearly disappeared inside the dirty old parka that used to hang in my back barn. Eyes as blue as a winter sky glared out at me from the dirt.

I squatted down in front of him. "Who are you?"

The boy blinked. Shrank away.

"I'm not going to hurt you. This is my farm. Where do you live?"

Still no answer. Just a little frown. I patted Chevy. "This is Chevy, and she

likes you. My name is Rick—Cedric Elvis
O'Toole."

Cedric was my mother's idea of class,
and Elvis was her one and only true love.
But the name has got me a lot of laughs
over the years, so I hoped I'd get at least a
smile from the boy. No such luck. He just
hugged Chevy to him. "Are you hungry?"
I asked, pretending to search my pockets.
"I've got soup back at the farm. And cheese
and eggs."

The kid stole a peek over his shoulder.
Like he was looking for something and
didn't want me to know. But he didn't say
a word.

"I'm going to call you Robin," I said.
"After Robin Hood. I used to pretend this
was Sherwood Forest when I was your age.
What? About eight?"

The boy rose to the bait. "Ten," he shot
back.

So he could talk after all. I stood up and held out my hand. "Okay, Robin. Let's go get you some soup. And I have a better jacket than that too."

Robin stood up. He didn't take my hand, but when I signaled to Chevy, at least he followed along.

Two

By the time we got back to the farmhouse, sunset had stolen all the heat out of the air. I was shivering. Robin trailed about twenty feet behind me, but when he saw the house, he stopped to stare, like he'd never seen it in the daytime. Now, I admit my house is a funny sight. Two walls are painted turquoise and the other two orange, because that's what was handy. Both paints were rejects from someone else's bad mix jobs—kind of like me.

At first Robin wouldn't even come up the front steps. Instead he headed for the barn,

sending the hens squawking in all direc-
tions. So I told him I was going inside to
feed Chevy, and soup would be ready in a
few minutes. When I peeked outside again,
he was down by the barn, feeding the hens.
I could see him smiling at them. But when
I called to him, the smile disappeared.

Even when my mother had remembered to feed me, she was never much of a
cook. So early on I'd figured out how to use
a stove and grow a few vegetables. My soup
wasn't fancy, but the smell was enough to
get Robin inside the house. He took the
bowl off the table and curled up on the
kitchen floor beside Chevy. He emptied his
bowl even faster than the dog would have.
I put a refill on the table, but he took it
down onto the floor too.

"Where are you from?" I asked.

He shrugged. I asked his name again.
Same shrug. I took the receiver off my wall
phone. It's a rotary type that earns me lots of

laughs, but after a few tweaks, it works just fine. His eyes followed every move I made.

"Your family will be worried about you," I said. "I better call the police."

I was hoping to reach Jessica Swan. She's a constable with our local detachment, and she has a soft spot for underdogs. She might know how to help this kid without dragging in her boss. But as soon as I said *police*, Robin lunged for the door. I grabbed his arm and dragged him back to the table.

"You can't go out there. It's cold. There are coyotes and bears looking for food for the winter."

"Not scared."

I looked at him. He glared back. He did seem scared, although not of the coyotes. "Are you lost?" I asked.

He shook his head.

"Did you run away?"

He looked down. Didn't answer. Now, I'm not much good at conversation. It was just my mother and me on the farm until she died, and I spent most of my childhood with imaginary friends. Sometimes I go all week without talking to anyone except turnips and goats. Now here I was with this kid in my kitchen, filthy and scared, but silent as a mule. I'd been there myself a few times.

I found a map in the drawer and spread it out. I traced some of the squiggly lines on the map. "This is Madrid County, where we are. Here's my farm, and here's Lake Madrid village, about three miles away. Over here is the woods where I found you."

He squinted at the map like he'd never seen anything like it. I moved my finger farther away. "Over here is North Grenfield, up here Ossington County. Can you see where you live?"

He ran his finger across the words. I pointed to the biggest town in the area. "Here?"

He lifted the paper to peer under it, like his house was hiding somewhere underneath. I had a sudden brainwave. Maybe the kid had never seen a map before. I pointed to the town's name. "Can you read this?" I asked.

"Read?"

I grabbed a pencil and printed the word *ROBIN* in big letters along the edge of the map. "What does that say?"

His eyes widened, and he reached for the pencil. "What this?"

He had an odd accent, like he didn't speak English well. He didn't sound French either. I told him it was a pencil. "You write with its tip."

He tugged at the tip. "How it come out?"

"Like this." I took a piece of charcoal from the fireplace and made a black line across the map. By now the map was becoming quite a mess.

He gripped the pencil in his fist, wrong way up, and tried to run it along the page. I turned it over and watched as he drew marks on the page. He began to smile as he scribbled and swirled. Not only had this kid never seen a map. He'd never even held a pencil!

Was he slow? Was that why he was wandering around lost in the woods? I remembered some old games my mother used to play with me, before she gave up hoping I'd be a doctor. I took two cherry tomatoes off the windowsill. "How many tomatoes are there?"

"Two."

I added four more. "Now how many?"

"Five."

"Count them."

He pouted. I started with the first tomato. "One, two...Now you."

"Three, four, five and five."

I wrote all the numbers down. "Which number is five?"

He picked up one of the tomatoes. I pointed to the number four. I had to be sure. "Give me this many tomatoes."

He picked up all six tomatoes and gave them to me, smiling as if he'd figured out the game. I counted them aloud and then pushed two back to his side. He ate them. In spite of myself, I laughed.

"You're still hungry."

He ate three eggs and four slices of toast. I was just beginning to think he was a bottomless pit when he laid his head on the table and fell fast asleep. I studied his smudged face and callused little hands. Now what? I thought. Call the police? This was more than just a missing kid. This was a mystery kid who could barely speak and had never even learned to count.

But he was still just a kid. It didn't seem fair to haul him off in a cruiser in the dead of night. That had happened to me, more than once, and I knew how scary it felt.

So I figured everything could wait until the morning, once he'd had a good night's sleep in a warm bed.

I carried him upstairs to my mother's old bedroom. No one had slept in it in fifteen years. Her room was just the same, if you didn't count the inch of dust. Her velvet Elvis still hung on the wall over her bed. Her shiny, hand-tooled red cowboy boots still sat on the floor by her dresser. There was a dusty box of shotgun shells on the cedar chest, beside the outline of her shotgun in the dust. But I suspected the kid had slept in worse places. The bed was comfy, and he barely opened an eye when I tucked a couple of old blankets over him.

That's when I noticed how filthy his sweater was. Dark stains smeared the front and cuffs. I touched them with my fingertips. They were dry and crusty. Mud? I sniffed. Sweat and barnyard manure. Carefully I pulled the sweater over his head, filled the sink with warm, soapy water and sank the sweater into the bubbles. The dirt softened. As it dissolved, it turned the water deep red.

I jerked back. A chill shot down my spine. The boy's clothes were soaked in blood.

I scrubbed and rinsed until the water ran clear. I peeked in on him again before I went to bed. He looked peaceful. Unhurt. The sweater looked as if it had never been washed. The blood could have been there for years, I told myself.

So I climbed into my own bed and tried not to think about it.

three

I thought he'd slept for a week. But when I got up the next morning to milk the goat, he was already gone. He had slipped out of the house without a sound, taking with him the red cowboy boots, the eggs from my fridge and the box of shotgun shells from the cedar chest.

Maybe not so slow after all.

• • •

"Your hens stop laying all of a sudden?" Aunt Penny asked. She was watching me unload the box of produce I had brought to her store. Since the October frosts started, the box was getting lighter. I still had some squash and apples worth selling. But most of my cash came from the eggs and goat's milk Aunt Penny sold from her private fridge at the back of the store. Enough people want my organic, free-range products that they don't let a few food regulations stand in their way.

Or maybe they just don't want to get on the wrong side of Aunt Penny. She's watched over the village from her store at the crossroads as long as folks can remember. There isn't a secret she doesn't know. She squinted at me now through her crooked gold glasses like she could read my every guilty thought. I thought of saying my fridge had broken down, but in the end I told her about Robin. Not about the blood or the box of ammo he'd stolen. Just about my taking him home the night before. That was bad enough.

"Ricky!" she said. "What were you thinking! You should have called the police right away!"

"But…" How could I tell her about the fear in the kid's eyes? "I don't think he wants to be found," I muttered.

"Doesn't matter. His family must be worried sick."

I wasn't so sure. What kind of parent doesn't even teach their kid to count? Even my mother had managed that. "If they cared, they'd be looking for him. I don't know anyone that's missing a kid. Have you heard anything?"

She shook her head. She'd been rearranging my squash on the shelves, and she stopped to rub her shoulder. No one really knows how old Aunt Penny is. She's actually my mother's aunt, and she's had gray hair as long as I can remember. And every year she gets a bit more stooped. The work is getting hard on her, but she'll be too stubborn to give up the store until she is ready for a pine box.

"Maybe his family's not from around here," she said. "The police will know. Speak of the devil..."

As if by magic, the bell over the front door rang. Our detachment commander, Sergeant Hurley, swaggered into the store. He was flashing his friendly neighborhood-cop grin, but he can spot a lawbreaker a mile away. I'm no good at lying, especially to him. My red face and tangled tongue give me away every time. So I ducked my head and mumbled hello as I scrambled out the door.

Driving past his cruiser, a much better idea hit me. Madrid County doesn't have much of a police force, so if the boss was out doing his rounds, Constable Jessica Swan might be alone at the station. She would at least listen to my story before heading out with sirens blaring. Jessica is still a newcomer by Lake Madrid standards, and she's about the only woman under fifty who doesn't think I'm a joke. Just thinking about her, my heart raced.

Since the detachment serves the whole county, it has a fancy new building on the main highway, about a mile outside of town. Jessica was on the phone when I arrived, but her sunny blue eyes lit up. I grew hot and my thoughts all disappeared. By the time she hung up, I'd only found about half of them. I wanted to be cool, but that's not my strong suit at the best of times.

"Working hard?" I asked, pointing to her computer.

She grinned. "Why? You got another body for us, Rick?"

I wished I could think of a funny come-back. I admit a couple of dead bodies have come my way, causing some teasing by the regulars at the Lion's Head. But it's not like I go looking. I tried to smile back. "Not today," I said. "But maybe something else. Has anyone reported stuff being stolen from their farms?"

Her smile faded. "What kind of stuff?"

"Small stuff. Vegetables, blankets." I kept quiet about the ammo. I'd seen no gun in the cave, and maybe the boy didn't know what the shells were for.

"You want to make a report, Rick?"

"No! I can't be sure. Maybe it's just kids. Any reports of kids causing trouble?"

She frowned like she was trying to see through me. I plowed on before she could see too much. "If it's just a joke, it's no big deal. But if a kid is in trouble, like maybe lost or ran away…"

"We have no reports of local children lost or missing."

"But how would you know? I mean, if they're from away? Or their family is just passing through?"

She waved her hand at her computer. "We get alerts from all across the country. And we pay attention to them. A missing child is a priority call."

"So, no alerts?"

"Is this serious, Rick? Are you saying you have reason to believe a child is missing?"

I was going to have to lie, and I hated doing that. Jessica is my friend, and I don't have too many of those. "I'm just checking. The nights are getting cold. But if there are no alerts..." I let my voice trail off.

She was still studying me, so I kept my eyes on the corkboard on the wall. It was covered with notices, including one about the village's pumpkin-carving contest. But nothing about a missing child. She turned to her computer and began to fiddle with her mouse. She started shaking her head. "Nothing new province- or nationwide," she said finally. "And no reports of thefts or trespassing in the neighboring counties either. Do you want to make a report?"

I was already backing out the door, afraid I'd said too much. Jessica is a softie, but she isn't stupid. I needed to protect Robin. Nobody had cared enough to teach him or even to report him missing. Living by his wits was the only life he knew. Before I got him in more trouble, I needed to find out why.

Four

There was no way to sneak up to my farm unnoticed. For one thing, my truck tires made an awful racket on the gravel road, and for another, a big cloud of dust trailed me down the road. So I was just turning in the gate when I spotted Robin running out of my barn. I skidded the truck to a stop by the barn and jumped out to chase him. As he ran, he dropped the armload of boards he was carrying.

I tackled him halfway up the first hill. He landed a couple of good kicks before

I pinned him to the ground. From inside his jacket, I pulled out my two best towels.

"Robin! What's going on?"

We both gasped for breath. He glared at me.

"Why are you hiding?"

"Not hiding."

"Then tell me who you are and where you live."

His chin wobbled, but he didn't answer.

"Then let's go. We're calling the police."

"No!"

"You can't steal from me. It's wrong. I'm trying to help you!"

"Sorry." He struggled to get free. "No police!"

"But you can't just stay in the woods. Winter's coming."

"I stay with you. On farm." He looked at me, his blue eyes huge. "Please."

"You can't stay with me. You're a kid."

"I strong. I help. I know farm."

I thought of all the trouble that could cause. Not just with his parents, who might be missing him, but with Aunt Penny and Jessica Swan. I would have to lie to all of them. I could feel him shivering beneath me, and I loosened my hand on his arm.

He grabbed my coat. "Please. No police. I promise not steal."

He was dirty, cold and scared. Something terrible must have happened to this boy. Something that had made his home worse than living rough in the woods. I didn't know what it was, but I could buy us both some time. Time for him to calm down. Time for me to figure out what to do.

I tried to sound fierce. "You promise you won't run away again?"

Tears filled his blue eyes. "Yes. Promise."

"And you'll give me back my shotgun shells?"

His wet eyes flickered. I tightened my grip. He looked away. Gave just the tiniest nod.

What have I done? I thought as I led him home again.

• • •

This time I ran him a bath. While I handed him clean clothes, I secretly checked his body. No scars, no wounds. I didn't ask him about the blood. For now, I needed to build some trust. I even put clean sheets and an extra blanket on the bed in the hopes he'd feel safe.

But the next morning the bed was empty. The blankets and pillow were gone. I swore out loud. "The kid has just blown his last chance," I grumbled as I headed out to the barn. I was surprised to see fresh straw in the chicken coop and clean water in the old laundry tub I used as a trough. Even the goat had been fed and milked.

Robin, however, was nowhere in sight.

Back inside, I found half a loaf of bread missing. But there was a bowl of fresh eggs and a pail of goat's milk on the counter. Also on the counter were the pencil and the map I had shown him the first night. It was even more scribbled on than before. Curious, I studied the scribbling. I saw that he had been practicing straight lines, curves and angles, and in the end had made an R. Sort of.

Had this kid been up half the night?

Hoping he'd come back, I fixed some breakfast for him and me. Then I drew up a couple of estimates for small jobs that were going to keep me afloat through the winter. It was almost noon when I packed up the eggs, milk and a couple more squash from the garden and signaled Chevy into the truck. I scanned the fields one last time, but they were empty. I couldn't put off Aunt Penny any longer.

The O'Tooles were never much for family even when my mother was alive. Aunt Penny was the only one still speaking to her after I was born. I guess being sixteen and pregnant without a man in sight didn't go over well with my mother's clan. But Aunt Penny was the O'Toole patron saint of lost causes. Even after my mother died, Aunt Penny figured she was all that stood between me and the wrong path.

Lake Madrid was mostly a cottage town, with a jumble of houses and stores strung along the lake. During the summer cottage season, the store kept Aunt Penny too busy to pay much attention to me. But now that most of the cottages were closed up for the winter, she had more time for her favorite lost cause.

Before I even opened my mouth about Robin, she saw right through me. She took a long look at the ice cream and popcorn in my order before she rang it through. I'm not big on junk food, but Robin needed a few pounds on him. And I needed something besides vegetables and eggs to fill that bottomless pit.

"You got an extra mouth to feed, Ricky?"

I mumbled something about liking ice cream on the apple pie she gave me. Then I slipped a notebook and a box of crayons onto the counter. Her eyebrows shot up.

I shrugged. "For a job."

She studied me. "You want to be careful, Ricky. A certain pretty blond constable might not be pleased."

Five

I was redder than a fire engine as I got back into my truck. Even I know Jessica Swan is way out of my league. She is a smart cop with the whole world open to her. What would she ever see in a bumbling country handyman like me? A grade-eleven education, a collection of junk and a falling-down house? That doesn't stop me from dreaming, but I don't want the whole village to know.

I felt pulled apart. By Robin, by Penny, by what Jessica would think of me. I knew I shouldn't keep this from her, but I'd made a promise to the kid. By the time I reached home, I was mad at everybody. Most of all myself. But Chevy leaped out of the truck, all excited. Usually she romps around with her tail waving, eager to check out the rabbits in the back field. But this time she headed instead toward one of the little sheds far from the house. Most of my sheds were so full of junk, you could hardly open the door. But this one still had some free floor space.

The door was shut. When I pushed it open, sunlight poured into the darkness, across a faded plaid blanket on the floor. I could see a bump beneath the blanket and long tangled hair on the pillow. Robin was fast asleep, but he bolted up when the sunlight hit. He shrank into the corner and looked at me with huge eyes. For a minute it looked like he didn't know where he was.

"Robin," I said, squatting down beside him. "You don't have to hide out here."

Chevy licked his face, and slowly he stopped looking scared. I picked up the pillow and blanket and started back to the house. I'd learned words didn't help. The boy would either follow, or he wouldn't.

He followed. Head down, fingers locked in Chevy's fur. "Thanks for taking care of the hens and the goat," I said once we were in the kitchen. I unpacked the groceries.

"I know farm."

"Yes, you do. Next time"—I opened the door to the fridge to put the food away— "you put the eggs and milk in here."

He peered inside. Opened all the compartments. "Okay."

I moved around the kitchen, showing him the stove, the toaster, the lights that came on at the flick of a switch. By the end, he was grinning as he turned the lights on and off.

I tried to sound casual. "You have no lights in your home?"

He nodded. "With match."

What century had this boy lived in? I took the notebook and crayons out of the bag and put them on the table. He flipped through the blank pages, frowning. While the soup warmed up, I printed the letter *R* on the first blank page. Then *O-B-I-N*.

"Robin," I said and pointed to the space below. "You try."

He took the crayon in his fist and made his first line. How did I teach a ten-year-old kid to read? Teachers had tried every trick in the book with me, and most of them hadn't worked. So who did I think I was? While I puzzled over that, Robin copied his name. Badly. Before I could say a word, he scribbled over it and started again underneath. By the time the soup was hot, he'd filled the whole page.

I remembered the silly books my mother used to read me. *Cat in the Hat. One Fish, Two Fish.* Maybe I should look for them upstairs. I also remembered the lists of rhymes from my remedial books. I'm not much good at reading, but I'm pretty good at drawing. So while we sat at the table eating our soup, I drew pictures and printed letters underneath. *A* for apple, *B* for bowl, *C* for cup, *T* for table. The rhyming words *cat, hat, bat, rat.*

Robin tried. Furrowed his brow and mouthed the sounds. But he couldn't get it. I cut words out and taped them around the kitchen. Another trick my mother had tried. *Chair* on the back of the chair. *Can* on the tomato soup. *Table, stove, fridge.* By the end of an hour, the room was filled with bits of paper. I made up his bed again and left him with some yard chores before I headed out to my job.

When I got back, the yard was swept. The dead tomato vines were cleared. The vegetable garden was filled with compost from my pile nearby. I found Robin in his favorite shed, surrounded by chains, clamps and springs. My old bear trap sat on the floor, half taken apart. He shrank away at the sight of me.

"Not steal! I make same."

I squatted beside him. He'd made a good start. But he needed more tools, including a blowtorch, to finish the job. I wasn't about to let him try that. My house might not be much, but I'm kind of attached to it.

That night after I put him to bed, I noticed the notebook open on the kitchen counter. I leafed through it. Robin had filled the entire book. First with copied letters and words, later with the numbers I had written on the map that first night. At the back, he'd made drawings of dogs, chickens, goats and trucks. He'd tried all the colors. Not much to look at, but the kid had never held crayons before. Whatever he was, he was not stupid.

I studied the drawings carefully, hoping for a clue to his past. There was only one. A small one-story house that looked nothing like mine. It had a front porch with what looked like a rocking chair on it. It wasn't much, but it was a start. Was it time to tell Jessica the truth? And get this kid back home with some real help?

Instead, I stalled. I admit, I kind of liked his company—and his help. I had a busy couple of days paneling the living room in a cottage near the village. So Robin was left to do the chores and keep himself busy. He spent hours in my junk sheds, fiddling with things. He played with Chevy and the goat, even enjoyed watching the hens. But he hardly talked. Every night I put him to bed in my mother's bed, and every morning I found him asleep in the shed. He ate like a football player, but during the night food still disappeared. Not only food, but my mother's sweaters, more towels and spare cushions from the couch.

So one night I woke up at 2:00 AM and went to peek in my mother's room. Sure enough, the bed was empty. I peered out the window. The moon was on the wane but still cast enough pale light that I could see a shape running toward the woods. Toward the mystery cave I had found a few days earlier.

What the hell was this boy up to?

Six

The next morning, mist rose off the frosted ground. I could see my breath, and I shivered as I went out to the barns. Winter was coming. I found the animals fed and Robin fast asleep in his shed. He didn't even stir. Whatever he had been up to in the night, it sure had worn him out.

I tiptoed out without waking him and signalled to Chevy. Together we set off across the field in the direction I'd seen Robin go. Chevy led the way, tail waving and nose to the ground. After a while we came to the cave. It was deserted. There was no microwave, no blanket on the floor or branch across the entrance. No sign of the things he'd been stealing either. Obviously, he had another secret place. I tried to remember the route we had taken when I first found him. Across the stream and deeper into the woods.

I ducked and wove my way forward. Slipping on moss and clambering over roots. Finally, I recognized the hill where I had caught up with him that first day. Found the rock he'd tried to hide behind. I stood on the spot, squinting through the trees. The leaves were all gone now, so I could see farther. I listened. Chevy stood still too, her nose twitching.

Nothing. Just crows squawking, squirrels chattering and wind scraping through the branches. I waited. Chevy turned, and her ears perked up. A low growl bubbled in her throat.

I held my breath. Bears were on the move right now, finding food and shelter for the winter. Their cubs would be playing nearby. Suddenly Chevy barked and took off farther up the hill. I shouted, but she ignored me. I scrambled after her, hoping she wasn't leading us both toward a mother bear. Up ahead I could hear her barking, a high-pitched warning bark. I followed the sound, my heart pounding. Over the hilltop and down the other side. Toward a mossy stream and another rocky overhang where I knew animals liked to gather. A pile of rocks and old boards made a sort of shack.

Chevy was standing by the rocks, barking. Her hackles up and her tail stiff. I could see nothing in the darkness inside. No black shape, no shiny teeth.

But it smelled like a rotting corpse.

I shrank back, afraid to look. Then I saw one of my towels draped over a tree branch to dry. And my blanket over another. My microwave was down by the stream.

The kid's secret lair! I rushed forward, slipping on the mossy rocks and falling head first into the darkness. I landed on my hands and knees on something soft. A cry startled me, and I yanked my hands back. I looked down, my eyes gradually getting used to the gloom. I saw my horse blanket on the floor and a pile of towels and blankets in front of me. The pile moved. It moaned. I reached up to pull the covers back. Saw a woman's face, white and shiny with sweat. Her eyes were shut and her lips cracked. She panted like a dog. The rancid stink rose from her.

I tugged on the blanket to drag her out into the light. Her eyes flew open. Glassy and unseeing, but as blue as a winter sky.

Robin's eyes.

Out in the sunlight, I could see how sick she was. Fever and stench radiated from her. I reached down to gather her into my arms. She weighed less than a hundred-pound sack of potatoes, but the trek through the woods was going to be hard. I grunted as I turned around.

And came face to face with the barrel of a shotgun. Robin blocked the path, his feet apart and both arms holding a shotgun almost as big as him.

"Help me, Robin. She's very sick."

"I help her."

"You can't. I can't. She needs a doctor."

"I use moss. She tell me."

"Is she your mother?" It might explain why no one was looking for him.

"My sister."

I looked at the woman's feverish face. At the cracked lips and furrows of pain. Illness had aged her.

"We need to get her home. It's too cold out here."

He shook his head wildly. The gun wavered. He tightened his grip in defiance.

"Robin, she will *die* out here!"

His chin quivered. "No doctor. No police."

I thought fast. One step at a time. "Okay," I said. "No doctor. But let me take her home, where I can see what's wrong with her."

Robin stared at the girl. She had fainted again and lay limp in my arms. He took a few quick breaths. Trying to gather his courage. And then he stepped aside.

Seven

"Aunt Penny, I need your help. Out at the farm."

"Is it the boy?"

"No. Yes. Sort of. Can you come quick?"

There was silence on the line. I hoped she heard how scared I was and would save the tongue-lashing for later. Robin and I had put his sister in my mother's bed and given her some water. But she was burning up. Way too sick for me to figure out. Maybe I should have called the doctor, but I turned to the next best thing. Robin didn't know. He was upstairs with her.

When he met Aunt Penny, I hoped he'd thank me.

Luckily, Aunt Penny can recognize real trouble. She said she'd close the store and come. I told her to bring all the medical supplies she had on the shelves.

She turned up with almost a whole drugstore. Aspirins, flu medicine, vapor rub, antiseptics, antibiotics, bandages and tape. I didn't ask her where she got it all. She caught one whiff of the mystery woman and snapped her fingers at me.

"She has an infection. Get me all the cloths, cold water and ice you can spare, Ricky. We've got to get the fever down."

Robin was hanging around the doorway, wide-eyed. She glared at him. "What happened to her?"

He just shook his head. Too scared to answer. I brought the ice and towels. Aunt Penny tossed the blankets on the floor and began pulling off the girl's jacket. She howled. Aunt Penny turned instead to her trousers. She peeled off the fleece outer layer and then the long johns. The girl's legs were like sticks. Aunt Penny sponged the sweat and dirt from her face and her neck. Then she laid a cold compress on her forehead and tilted her head to give her some water. She slipped a couple of pills into her mouth. The girl made a face. Shook her head weakly.

Aunt Penny washed her legs in the cool water and tried again to touch her jacket. The girl jerked away. Penny leaned toward her. "I have to take off your jacket, dear."

I'd never heard my aunt talk so gently. Seen her touch so softly. The girl said nothing, but whimpered as Aunt Penny slowly removed her clothes. First a jacket, then a sweater of my mother's and finally a fleece soaked with dirt, blood and rot. Underneath was one of my towels, stained yellow and black. The stink grew so strong I held my nose. Robin shook all over.

Finally, the wound was exposed. A raw purple hole in her side, partly healed but oozing yellow pus. Aunt Penny pursed her lips. She leaned in and sniffed. Shot a glance at Robin.

"Spruce gum. Who taught you that?"

Robin thrust out his chin. "She tell me."

I knew what Aunt Penny was thinking. Spruce gum was traditional Indian medicine. Were these kids part Native? Or had they been raised on an isolated reserve? Robin clearly wasn't saying, and Aunt Penny didn't push it. Instead, she touched his arm.

"Well, it helped, but it's not enough. Ricky, get me hot water and the antiseptic soap."

I brought a big bowl. Gave her more clean cloths. Watched as she dabbed at the wound. The girl shrieked.

"Hold her hands," Penny said. She stayed so calm. Slowly she soaked away the dried pus and blood. Washed it again and again. Dried it. Poured alcohol over it and then peered at it. In the long silence, there was nothing but the girl's moans.

Then Aunt Penny turned on Robin, no longer soft. "This is a bullet hole. Ricky, call the police."

"No!" It was the girl who shrieked. Loud. Fierce. I stopped halfway to the door.

"You've been shot," Penny said. "You need a doctor."

"No, you fix it."

"I can't fix it."

"No doctors. No police. Please!"

The girl spoke English better than Robin, but with the same odd accent. She was trying to sit up, and the wound was oozing again. Aunt Penny tried to calm her.

"You have to stay still."

"No police! Promise!"

"Okay. For now. I will wash the rest of you and bandage this so you can rest."

Aunt Penny sent Robin and me away while she finished up. When she finally came downstairs, I was preparing chicken soup. She tried to be gentle with Robin, but I knew she was angry. Maybe even scared. Not much scares Aunt Penny.

"Someone shot your sister, Robin. I think the bullet went straight through, but it's not healing well. This is serious."

"An accident. A hunter, in woods. Shooting at deer."

"It's not deer-hunting season yet."

Robin froze.

"The police must—"

"No! Please! Accident, is all. I clean. I take good care."

Aunt Penny gave him a long look. Her lips were tight. But she kept her voice soft. "Yes, you did, dear. Now take this soup up to her."

After he'd gone, she reached for the phone.

I dived to stop her. "What are you doing!"

"Calling Jessica Swan."

"But..." I sputtered. Floundered. "You promised him—"

"I promised him nothing. There's more to this. That little slip of a girl up there? She's borne a child."

Eight

I stared at her. "How can you tell?"

"There are signs."

Her expression said "don't ask," so I didn't. I looked for a different route. "So what? Is that a crime?"

"No, but Children's Services has to be involved."

My heart jumped. I hate Children's Services. Sometimes my mother would get really bad, and they'd decide she wasn't taking care of me. They'd stick me in foster care. I pictured Robin in foster care. In a strange home, a real school. With all the kids laughing at his accent and calling him a retard.

"But we don't know what happened to her baby," I said. "We don't know how old she is. Maybe she's eighteen!"

"But the boy, at least, is underage. You can't keep him here, Ricky. And let's face it, these kids haven't been exactly truthful."

I stepped between Aunt Penny and the telephone. Spread my arms. She gave me a long stare. I'd never stood up to Aunt Penny before. Or to Children's Services. I'd never stood up for my mother either. She hadn't been much good at mothering, but she was all I'd had.

"Then let's ask them," I said. "Give them a chance to tell us the truth."

She took a long time to decide. Finally, she turned around and marched up to the bedroom. Robin was spooning soup into Marian's mouth. Neither one would tell us their names, so that's what I had decided to call her, to go with Robin. She looked half-dead, but she was eating.

"You realize I have to call Children's Services," Aunt Penny said. Never one to pull punches. "Robin is underage. He needs care. Proper schooling."

Marian's eyes flashed. "I take care of him."

"But you're a child yourself. The two of you—"

"I am not a child. I am twenty-two."

"And the baby you had?"

Marian dropped her gaze. She pushed Robin aside and murmured to him in another language.

"But—" he began.

"Go!"

"He is not my brother," she said when he had left. I heard his footsteps dragging on the stairs. I figured he'd be listening.

"I didn't think so," Aunt Penny said to Marian. "He's your son."

There was no sound from the stairs. Marian turned pink. "He doesn't know. This is the story we tell."

"Who's we?"

She struggled to sit up. To face Aunt Penny straight on. "I am adult. Old enough to take care of him."

Aunt Penny was shaking her head.

Marian sagged. "Please. That is what is important."

"You are sick."

"No law. No police." Tears stood in her eyes. She looked so pale I thought she'd faint.

"We'll talk tomorrow," I said. I wanted to drag Aunt Penny out of there. But luckily, I didn't need to. She felt Marian's forehead, tightened her lips and headed out of the room without another word.

She saved those up for me the minute we got downstairs. "Those kids need help," she hissed. "That girl could die without a doctor."

"But you gave her the antibiotics."

"*My* antibiotics. Two years old. Something's not right here, Ricky. Even if that girl is twenty-two, that means she was a child when the boy was born. That's child abuse. Somewhere out there, a sex criminal is walking free—"

"But…" I couldn't think of an answer. She was right. It was probably why the kids were running away.

"There's no but. We'll let her sleep tonight, but in the morning I'm going to Jessica Swan. This is out of your hands, Ricky."

I knew I wasn't going to budge her. She slept on the sofa in the front room, like she was guarding the door. Robin slept on the floor in Marian's room, too scared to let her out of his sight. None of us slept very well, and when I got up, Aunt Penny was already getting ready to head into town.

I didn't want her going by herself. I didn't want to leave the kids in the farmhouse alone either, but someone had to stand up for them. I knew what it was like to have the police and child welfare swoop in. Like hawks. Fast. Powerful. And ruthless.

The police detachment was quiet when Aunt Penny and I arrived. Jessica Swan was on the front desk, and so my fear was mixed with thrill. She had a coffee at her side and a report in front of her. But she gave us a big smile as she shoved it aside.

"You're up early! Want some coffee?"

I knew I had to jump in before Aunt Penny did. "That missing kid I was talking about—" I started.

Surprise replaced the smile. "I've kept an eye open, Rick. There have been no missing-child reports. Or thefts."

"They're at my farm. I mean, he's at my farm. With his sister. I mean, his mother."

I could feel my ears burning. I tried to untangle my words before Aunt Penny could jump in. "She's hurt."

Aunt Penny jumped in anyway. "We need a doctor and Children's Services."

"Not Children's Services," I said. "The mother is old enough—"

"She wasn't when she conceived the boy," Aunt Penny snapped. "And the boy is neglected. Raised like an animal in a barn. No schooling, no manners. He can barely speak English."

Jessica had been staring at us in amazement. "First things first. The woman. How bad is she?"

"Getting better," I said.

"She has a bullet hole—"

"A bullet hole!" Jessica leaped up. "Why didn't you say—"

At that moment the door to the commander's office flew open. "Did I hear *bullet hole*?" Sergeant Hurley said. He looked from Jessica to Penny to me. "No one's going anywhere until you tell me what the hell is going on!"

Nine

For once I was happy to see Sergeant Hurley. He'd been handling trouble since before I was born, most of it in Madrid County. If anyone could take the reins from Aunt Penny, it would be him.

Instead of heading off with sirens blaring, he sat back and listened to my whole story from beginning to end. As he listened, my pulse came back to normal. He ordered Jessica to call the paramedics and double-check all the missing persons. Then he got up, hitched his belt and studied the big map on the wall. His eyes narrowed. His finger traced roads from my farm, finally stopping in a big area of bush farther north.

It was a region where many of the local guys had their hunt camps. I had never been up there because I don't like hunting. But I knew there was nothing but acres of lakes, forests and deer.

He tapped the area with his finger. "Pretty rough country up here. A hundred years ago it was heavily logged, but settlers couldn't make a go of farming. Too much rock and bush."

I thought of my own patch of scrub. Not much better down here, I almost said. But I didn't want to interrupt. Hurley didn't usually take me this seriously. In the background, Jessica spoke into the phone.

"But there are still some tough old-timers up there, making a go of it," Hurley said. "Survivalist types, loners, misfits. They like to run things their own way, don't like rules and regulations. You don't bother me and I won't bother you. And if they're doing no harm, we mostly leave them be."

"That's nearly thirty miles away! How did the kids get to my place?"

Hurley shrugged. "Walked? Hitched? Stowed away?"

I thought it over. It made a crazy kind of sense. The kids were smart enough. "The boy does act like he's never seen the outside world. Not even electricity."

Aunt Penny huffed. "So the authorities just ignored these kids? The girl was twelve years old when she had the boy, and he's never been in school."

Hurley shrugged. "Likely no one knew. The farms are pretty isolated, and these guys aren't exactly friendly with their neighbors. Lots of things—violence, abuse— go on in those remote homesteads that never get reported. Folks mind their own business."

"But the kids themselves. The girl. Why stay in that situation all those years?" Right and wrong always did seem clearer to Aunt Penny than to the rest of us.

Jessica hung up. "The paramedics are on their way from Hinchinbrooke, sir."

Hinchinbrooke was half an hour away over bad roads. Hurley made a face. "Call them back. Tell them we'll meet them out at Rick's place." He picked up his keys and strapped on his utility belt as he headed out the door. He gave Aunt Penny a patient look. "Where's a girl like that going to go?" he asked. "Who is she going to tell? And if this was her life, would she even know any different?"

Aunt Penny has never been married, never had a family. Has never known any life except her store and our town. But people tell her things over the counter. Even she knows about the things that go on behind closed country doors. When life's frustrations boil over, and guys come home from the Lion's Head full of too much booze and anger. For some wives, it is just the price to be paid for a home.

But Aunt Penny tightened her jaw as she followed him outside. She was not giving up on the kids just yet. "Well, it ends now. The woman may be of age, but she's in no condition to take care of him."

"Maybe when she's better—"

"Not because she's sick, but because she hasn't protected and nurtured him! He's little more than an animal. Not even the most basic instruction!"

"Inbreeding," Hurley said bluntly. "Not a whole lot of women to choose from up there. I bet her father or uncle is the father. Sometimes the children turn out retarded, and the family keeps them hidden at home." He stopped by his cruiser. Laid a hand on Aunt Penny's arm. "Let me do my job, Penny. Go home.

I'll take Rick back and make sure these kids are all right."

As we drove along the main highway toward my place, I could feel my heart pounding. I was angry at what he'd said but afraid to stand up to him.

Finally, I couldn't stand the silence any longer. "Robin is not retarded!" I burst out. "He's just never been to school. He knows a whole lot about tending a farm, and he's even learning to read."

"If he's never been to school, that's even worse," Hurley said. With a smooth hand he steered the cruiser off the main highway. "Your aunt is right. Children's Services has to be called in."

Dust rose around us from my back-country road. Far ahead, I could see my tin roof glinting in the sun. I knew I didn't have much time left to convince him. "He's scared enough already. There are so many new things. He knows me.

He knows the farm. If you drag in Children's Services..."

He looked over at me. Hurley had been a rookie cop the first time I was taken into care. He'd known my mother all her life. They'd been in high school together. He had tried to help her, but she'd been too lost in her own world. I think he always felt guilty about that. He's grown tougher over the years, but he still has kind of a soft spot for me. "Let's see what we've got first, okay?" he said.

I spotted the first hint of trouble as soon as we turned in the gate. The ambulance hadn't arrived yet, but Chevy was missing from her post on the front porch. I said nothing, but my heart jumped into my throat. Hurley parked by my truck and climbed out. He hitched his gun belt over his gut and headed for the door. I trailed, trying to plan my next move. The house was very quiet. Too quiet.

Without a word, Hurley headed upstairs. He aimed straight for my mother's bedroom, like he knew exactly where it was. I had to run to keep up with him. In the doorway, he stopped so fast that I bumped into him.

"Fuck," he muttered. I peered over his shoulder. Saw the bedding strewn on the floor, the bandages and pills all gone from the dresser. The bed empty.

Hurley spun on his heel and rushed back downstairs. His face was dark red. By the time he reached the kitchen, he was already on his radio to dispatch. "Now we've got trouble," he said. "They're missing."

I stood there in silence. Sick with fear. We had more trouble than Hurley knew. Because my mother's shotgun was not where I'd put it the night before.

Ten

By the time Sergeant Hurley left my farm, a full-scale cop alert had gone out. Hurley had taken the kids' dishes for fingerprinting and some bedding for hair samples. Maybe even DNA if it came to that. "The kids lied and ran away," Hurley said. "Even without the bullet hole, that's suspicious. We need to find out who they are."

I didn't dare tell him about the shotgun.

I knew the cops would question all my neighbors. And check cars up and down the highway. My heart was in my throat. There was no telling what Robin would do if he was cornered. I was the only person he trusted at all, and that wasn't saying much. But if I could find him first, there was a small chance I could stop a disaster.

When I was sure there were no cops around, I went into the woods to the hide-outs. I hoped Chevy was with them, as she would bark if I got close. No luck. The cave and the shack down by the stream were both empty. It looked like the kids had disappeared.

It was early afternoon when I got back home. Still no Chevy. That's when I noticed that the goat had been milked and the eggs collected. Some soup was missing from the fridge. Had Robin done all of this while I was at the police station that morning, or had he sneaked back just now, while I was out looking for him?

Even though I was worried, I felt some comfort. The kids might not be far away, and at least they had some food with them.

I got in my truck and headed to my neighbor's farm about a mile and half away. No, he hadn't seen anyone, he told me. He hadn't noticed anything stolen either. A cop had just been by, asking him the same questions.

The next neighbor had almost the same story. Buddy Bourke is too old to do any farming anymore. So he spends his days sitting on his front porch, watching the cars go by. Not much gets by him, but he hadn't seen the kids.

"My hatchet went missing a couple of weeks ago," he said. "But more than likely I just left it somewhere out in the bush."

His wife appeared in the doorway behind him. She is as bent and wrinkled as an old cornstalk. "Left your head out there too," she said. "But while you're here, Rick, that old snowmobile by the barn is yours for the taking if you can get it into your truck."

I could still hear her laughing as I drove off toward the next farm. Everyone knows I have half a dozen snowmobiles in my sheds already. And fourteen lawn mowers, plus washing machines, old fridges and more junk than I can count. I should probably say no more often.

The sun was almost down by the time I finally drove back through the village. I'd had no luck finding the kids. Aunt Penny was closing up. Tractors were returning to their barns. The parking lot of the Lion's Head was filling up. I'm not really big on beer and company, and I'd already had more conversation that day than I usually have in a week. But if anyone had heard any rumors, it would be the regulars at the Lion's Head.

The tables were full, and a hockey game was on over the bar. I ordered a half-pint and studied the guys at the nearest table. By themselves, they aren't too bad.

I've even done work for some of them. Fixing their snowmobiles, repairing their decks and stuff. But beer and hockey make them stupid. It didn't take long for the stupidest one, Desroches, to yell at me.

"Hey, Tool! I hear you had a couple of half-wit visitors. Kids from up north?"

I pasted on a smile and joined them. It was going to be tough going against these guys. They already had a table full of empty beer bottles. But I did it for Robin. "They've run off," I said. "The cops are looking for them. The girl's twenty-two, the boy ten. Any of you see them?"

"Why? They didn't pay their bill?"

"The girl needs medical attention. She's been shot."

Desroches grinned. He was on a roll. "It's called a gun, Tool. You don't go pointing it at people."

"She says a hunter did it."

That sobered them up a bit. Most of them are hunters, not always legally. "They're not from around here," I said. "They talk with accents."

Jack Ripley leaned forward. Jack is smarter than the others, and he was not as drunk. I had his interest. "French?"

I shook my head. An idea popped into my head as I looked at the TV. "More like a Russian hockey player."

"But with teeth, I hope," Jack said.

Laughter all around. Desroches winked. "Pretty girl?"

I shrugged. I never was any good at girl bragging, and all the guys know it.

"You'd notice her," I said. "She's got nice blue eyes."

"Eyes. *Oooh*."

The talk got even worse after that, so I drained my half-pint and got up. I was halfway out to my truck when the bar door opened and Jack Ripley came out.

Jack has a big dairy farm on the other side of the county, and he's too busy for serious drinking. He usually just comes for the company and the hockey game.

"Blue eyes?" he said.

I nodded. "Amazing blue eyes. Her brother has them too."

He squinted into the darkness. "I think I might know her."

My heart did a cartwheel. "Who is she?"

"You know our deer-hunt camp up in Ossington County? The one me and my brothers go to every fall?"

I know Ossington County. It's in the area Sergeant Hurley talked about—a rugged backcountry of forests and lakes about thirty miles north. Full of fish and game, but the people are dirt poor. Jack usually brings me a venison roast after the hunt. I'm not a fan of killing wild animals, but I can never say no to the venison roast either.

"I could be wrong," Jack said, "but she sounds like the camp cook we had the last couple of years. Her name was Donnie. She was skittish as a young colt, hardly spoke a word, hardly even looked you in the eye. But she did have an accent and really blue eyes. And we heard she was the daughter of a local hermit up there."

"Who?"

Ripley shrugged. "Never knew his name. We made the arrangement through the local store. Everyone just called him the Rooskie."

Rooskie! Russian. My hopes soared. "Do you know anything else? Where he lives?"

"Sort of. I drove her partway home once. She wouldn't let me take her all the way. But if you've got a map, I can show you the road."

Eleven

No Trespassing, the sign said in huge black letters. A branch scratched the side of my truck as I dodged a boulder in the road. I wouldn't actually have called it a road. More like an ATV track through deep forest. It seemed to go on forever. Farther up, another handmade sign. *Keep Out!*

I hoped the Russian didn't have a gun.

I'd left my farm bright and early in the morning, but the drive up to Ossington County had taken nearly two hours. The last nine miles had been nothing but mud and potholes, and now this overgrown track.

Soon I came to a six-foot steel gate, chained shut with a heavy padlock. But the lock hung open, so I got out to unwind the chain and push back the gate. A gleam of metal poking through the dry leaves caught my eye. I leaned over for a closer look. It was a bear trap, jaws open, waiting for an intruder. There was nothing humane about that trap. Its huge teeth were razor sharp. I froze in place. Peered around. More traps were buried in the road around the gate. I inched around them and watched every step as I tugged open the gate.

Finally, I drove through, expecting gunfire or attack dogs. Nothing but silent trees. Up ahead the forest opened into a wide clearing. On one side, two goats watched me curiously from a field of dried-out hay. Across the road was a vegetable garden, protected by strips of cloth that flapped in the wind. Pumpkins lay rotting on the ground, and dead tomato plants clung to the stakes.

The place made mine look like paradise. A jumble of buildings had been hammered together from refuse. Barn, chicken coop, a couple of sheds and an outhouse. Cats and chickens roamed in the dirt, and a skinny cow stared at me through sickly eyes.

At the back of the clearing stood a small log cabin with a rocking chair on its porch. The house Robin had drawn in the notebook. I was at the right place! I stopped the truck and climbed out, keeping my head down. Expecting bullets. The stink hit me right away. Rotting manure, unwashed barns, neglected animals. And something else.

As I looked closer, a chill ran down my spine. I had stopped only six inches from sharp spikes sticking out of the road. Ready to shred my tires. All the buildings, including the outhouse, had huge padlocks or chains on them. Who did this guy think would steal from him? And *what*?

The goats trotted over to me right away, and even the cats rubbed my legs. A water pump sat in the middle of the yard, but there was no water in the trough and no feed in the yard. No sign that anyone was taking care of the place.

I pumped some water into the trough. The animals crowded around and drank like they hadn't had water in days. I crossed the yard to the small barn, afraid of what I'd find. Animals dead or starving in their stalls? A thin wire had been strung across the doorway. I jerked back just before I strangled myself. What was it for? I wondered. To sound an alarm? Or, worse, to trigger a gun?

I ducked under it and went inside. The barn looked empty. I checked each stall. To my relief, they were all empty and neatly swept. Except the last one, where I found a bowl, cup, spoon and small bedroll tucked in the corner.

Just the way Robin kept his bed at my place.

I retraced my steps, ducked under the wire and headed to the main house. The windows were barred, the curtains drawn. I could see no signs of movement. Even so, I approached cautiously. Watched where I put my feet. Paused at each creak as I climbed the steps. There was another trip wire over the front door. Another heavy padlock. But this padlock was smashed, and the door was wide open. Beyond it, the curtained room was dark. I called out. No answer. I knocked. Still nothing.

I put my hand on the door and gave a gentle shove. Jumped back in case a shotgun was rigged to it. Nothing. Finally, I screwed up my courage and stepped inside.

Twelve

The house was one big room. It had an old black wood-burning cookstove, a table, and three chairs covered with hand-made quilts. The walls were rough logs, with straw and wood fiber shoved into the chinks to keep the wind out. The pine floor planks were dark with stains. More quilts hung on the walls, and the bright colors livened up the room. It felt simple and homey.

On the back wall, a curtain led to a small nook. I peeked in. A bed sat in the corner, neatly made with another quilt.

Beside it, a man's clothing hung on pegs. A big man, from the size of the overalls. A smaller shirt and trousers lay folded on a shelf under the window. A chamber pot sat on the floor under a washstand and pitcher. Two toothbrushes.

So Marian and the Russian slept together in here. Robin slept in the barn. I shivered, even though it wasn't cold. The place didn't feel so homey anymore. I turned back into the main room. That's when I saw the guns in the corner. Rifles and shotguns and pistols. At least a dozen of them were stored in a glass case, which was smashed open. Broken glass shone on the neatly swept floor. A box of .308 ammunition was ripped open, spilling cartridges onto the floor.

The .308 is a big-game rifle. Capable of bringing down a deer or a moose. Or a human. As my eyes got used to the dim light, I saw what I'd missed earlier. The stains on the floor were blood. Pooled by the bedroom door and streaked across the floor. Drag marks led out the door.

I slammed out of the house, my heart pounding. Leaned against the wall to catch my breath. As I sucked air into my lungs, I realized what the stink was.

Death.

The drag marks headed down the steps and around the side of the house. Someone had tried to scuff them out, but the gouges were deep. I stared at them for a long time. Some heavy object had dug two lines into the ground. I tried to think. The blood was dried. Marian and Robin had been on my land for almost a month. Whatever bad thing had happened here, it was not recent.

I should have called the police. But there was no phone. Not even electricity. This guy lived not only off the grid, but in another century. I should have jumped in my truck and got the hell out. Not stopped until I reached home. Or the nearest town.

I should at least have grabbed a gun.

But I followed the drag marks. Around the back of the house and into the woods behind. Up the hill. Tracking the deep gouges through fallen leaves. The smell grew so bad that I covered my nose. Took shallow breaths through my mouth. Almost stepped on a chunk of bone covered with flies. Up ahead, crows squabbled over something, black wings flapping. As I came closer, they took to the air in an angry whoosh. Leaving behind their prize.

What was left of a body, half buried under leaves. Arms missing, flesh stripped, flies buzzing in and out. Big boots were the only clue that it had once been a man.

thirteen

It was well past dark by the time I finally got back home. The Ossington County police had lots of questions but were not big on answers. When I showed up at the local detachment, babbling about murder, they didn't believe a word of my story. They thought I'd gone to the place to rob it. Or establish a grow-op. Or maybe I'd even killed the guy. They held me for hours, fingerprinted and photographed me. Just routine, they said, because I'd been at the scene. I was too freaked out for a snappy comeback. My tongue was in so many knots I could hardly get a word out.

Once I gave them Hurley's name, things got better. But they wanted to know all about Marian and Robin, and how I had learned about the Russian. My thoughts were whirling. Where was the Russian? Who was the dead man? The rifle case had been broken into. Robin had blood all over his clothes, and Marian had been shot. She and Robin had stolen my shotgun. No matter how I tried to fit these pieces together, I didn't like the picture. So I kept my answers short and let the cops do their own thinking. They weren't too happy about that. They finally let me go, but I figured my poor farm would be swarming with them by the time I got home.

I was relieved to see my house in darkness, with not a single cop car out front, when I drove up the lane. There was still no sign of Marian and Robin, but the animals had been tended to. Chevy was back home, fed and thrilled to see me.

I was especially happy to find a bag of carrots and some cheese missing from my fridge. I fell into bed, too tired to even undress. I was freaked and worried and relieved all at once. Whatever trouble the kids were in, they were staying near enough for me to help.

• • •

The next day I was on my third coffee when I spotted a cop car coming up my lane. I swore aloud. But when Jessica Swan climbed out, I tingled in spite of myself. Her blond hair shone in the morning sun as she scanned my fields. Luckily, neither kid was in sight. I put on my jacket and went outside.

She smiled at me. "Any more where that came from, Rick?" she asked, nodding at my coffee. She followed me inside. While I poured her a cup, she sneaked a glance down the hall. Around the kitchen. She smiled when she saw all the sticky labels, and I felt my cheeks flush. To cut her off, I led the way back outside, even though it was freezing out there. I prayed the kids would have the sense to stay out of sight with her cruiser parked in plain view.

We sat on the front steps in the sun. She wrapped her hands around the warm coffee cup and took a sip. Her arm brushed mine.

"Any sign of the two missing kids?" she asked.

"No," I said. I figured I'd leave it at that.

She didn't push it. "Things are looking bad, Rick. The coroner estimates the victim's been dead more than a month. Shot in the back. The investigating officers found a .308 Winchester in the barn that was recently fired. We won't know until the postmortem if it's the murder weapon. Or even if they can find the bullet. They brought in a forensics team from headquarters, and they've lifted a usable print from the rifle. Matched it to the cup and bowl in the barn."

All the air went out of my lungs. All the joy from the air. I couldn't talk. She looked at me sideways.

"They also found a bedroll in the barn. Didn't you say Robin preferred to sleep in your barn?"

Still I said nothing. She sipped her coffee. Poked at the dirt with her toe. Her voice grew soft. "There's a nationwide warrant out for their apprehension, Rick. Went out this morning. I thought you'd want to know."

"Poor kids," I managed.

"Yeah. It will take a while to put all the pieces together. To figure out what happened there. To the dead man, and to the kids."

"Do they know who it is?"

"The body itself?" She shook her head. "They'll have to go by dental records. Or DNA. After weeks in the bush, there's not much left of him."

"But the man who lived there? Do they know who he is?"

"No name yet. The cops are interviewing people in the area, but no one seems to know his real name. Just the nickname Rooskie, which they gave him because of his accent. We'll be trying to trace him through his fingerprints at the scene."

I finally felt on safer ground. "But what about land registry? Taxes?"

"He's a squatter. That back woodlot belongs to an old guy who's been in a nursing home for years. Completely gaga, and his son lives out west. No one's been on the property in years."

"But the neighbors knew he and the kids were there."

"They figured he was renting. No one asked any questions. You know how it is, Rick. Live and let live, especially up there. No one's going to bring in the authorities. The word was that he moved onto the place about ten years ago and kept to himself. He did tell one neighbor that his wife had died, leaving him with the two children to support. He was a back-to-the-land type, just wanted to be left alone."

I thought about Children's Services swooping down on my mother at every hint of trouble. "But what about school? Doctors?"

"He told people he was homeschooling them. He didn't trust authorities and was afraid of being investigated. Afraid his kids would be taken away. I think people up there can relate to that."

So could I. Still, I could feel my face growing hot with anger. "But he didn't even provide the basics. Robin wasn't even taught to read. He slept in a barn, fed like a dog!"

"But no one knew that. The few times people saw the family in the nearby town, there were no signs of trouble. They were poor, but the kids were clean. They didn't appear mistreated or unhappy. In fact, they all seemed to genuinely love each other."

"That doesn't make any sense! He was abusing her. And she says Robin is her son."

"Incest..." Jessica paused. She seemed to be trying to pick her words. "In some of these families, it seems natural. The girl might not have known any different. I'm not saying it's right. Just that to some abused kids it feels like a normal part of love."

"Then..." I was feeling stubborn. Still fighting the facts. "If they were happy together, there's no reason for the kids to shoot him."

"If the body is his. We don't know that yet." She paused again. "There is one more thing. There was a stranger, an American, reported in the vicinity a few weeks ago. He showed up in the village asking questions about a young woman with pale blue eyes living with a foreign man."

Fourteen

It was my day for visitors. People don't drive all the way out to my farm often, but suddenly there were two in one day. I was in the barn, working on an alarm system. I needed to keep my hands busy and my thoughts off those kids. The crazy Russian's trip wires and traps had given me an idea.

Aunt Penny's truck has needed a valve job for months, so I knew it was her coming up the lane. I watched as she climbed out and squinted all around, like she was looking for something. Most likely the kids.

"They're not here," I called, coming out of the barn.

She zipped her jacket tight and blew on her hands. "It's cold as Judgment Day today. Snow in the air."

I played along. "I better get your snow tires on. Are they in the truck?"

She shook her head. "Next time. I just came for the eggs."

Like hell, I thought. And before I could stop her, she was inside the house. For an old lady, she could move fast when she wanted to. She peered into my fridge, probably checking how many eggs I had. Which was none. Robin must have sneaked into the chicken coop before I got up.

She turned to me with a scowl. "I hope you're not doing anything foolish, Ricky. You're a long way from help out here."

The detachment was just three miles up the highway, but I knew that wasn't what she meant. "They're just scared kids,

Aunt Penny. Even if they were here, which they're not."

"Jessica Swan been out to see you?"

I nodded.

"Then you know what the cops found."

"I know what I found too. They lived with a crazy man. He had traps and trip wires and *Keep Out* signs all over the place."

She looked around my kitchen at all the sticky labels I'd put up. Her expression softened. "Ricky, I know they're scared kids, but that boy may also be a killer. We don't know what they've been through, but they may be dangerous. Especially if they're desperate. It was on the radio this morning that you found the body. You don't want to get caught in the middle."

There had been one nosy reporter outside the Ossington detachment when the cops had finally let me go. They must have told him who I was. Somehow, I had to convince Aunt Penny that Robin and

Marian were gone. Robin obviously trusted that I wouldn't betray them. "I won't be, Aunt Penny. They know better than to hang around here with all the cops snooping around."

"Jessica Swan is no fool," she said. "You don't want to be caught helping fugitives either. That could land you in jail."

She was looking in the sink now. Maybe checking for extra dishes. My cheeks grew hot, but I held my temper.

She must have noticed. Not much gets by her. When she headed back out to her truck, she glanced up at the sky. "I'm just doing you a favor, Ricky. The cops can use the satellites to spy on people now. And don't forget that bullet hole in the girl. Robin might have put it there."

I hadn't forgotten. I also hadn't forgotten my missing shotgun. I didn't tell her about it, of course, but after she left, I started worrying. I wasn't scared of Robin or Marian.

I knew those kids. I knew they wouldn't hurt me. But I did worry about what they'd do if the cops cornered them.

I didn't know where they were. I had checked their hiding places and found no trace of them. But I knew they were out there somewhere, close enough to sneak back to the farm for food. But they were all alone in the bush, maybe with nothing but a lean-to of cedar boughs to protect them.

Aunt Penny was right about one thing. Snow was coming. Winter, with its cold that gets into your bones. Robin and Marian might be afraid to light a fire in case the smoke tipped off the cops. Marian was still very weak. Even if Aunt Penny's antibiotics worked, it would be a long time before she recovered her strength. Living rough in the cold and damp could kill her yet.

And then there was the mysterious American. Who was he? What had he been up to? Was he the one lying dead in the woods? Was the crazy Russian on the loose, searching for his kids? No matter who was dead and who was still alive, it spelled danger for the kids. And I was the one who might have led that danger back here. Because of that nosy reporter, it might soon be all over the news that Cedric Elvis O'Toole had found the body. Not too many with that name in the phone book.

I went back into the barn to work on my trip wires. I'd never even needed locks on my front door, let alone an alarm system. I didn't have time now to get fancy. A few bicycle horns and floodlights would have to do. I strung wires and switches to the gate and across the lane. I put another for good measure by the front door. By the end of the day, I was pretty proud of the system. It would work even if an intruder got out of his car and sneaked around my gate.

Next, I went inside and heated up a big pot of stew. It wouldn't keep Marian and

Robin warm all night, but it would get them started. I filled some old thermoses with stew and hot tea, wrapped them in more blankets and left them down by the vegetable garden.

In the morning they were gone. I made more stew and tea the next night. That also disappeared, replaced by the empty thermoses. I never saw the kids. Never looked for them either. I was afraid that if they knew I was looking, they'd run away for good.

We were just getting into a rhythm, and I was beginning to relax, when a few nights later a blast of noise woke me from a dead sleep. Chevy leaped off the bed, barking.

My bicycle horn! I rushed to the window. The yard was lit up like high noon. A truck was racing back down the lane, fishtailing wildly. In the floodlights, it was easy to see the tailgate plastered with bumper stickers.

I couldn't make out any words, but I recognized the Confederate flag.

The American had come.

Fifteen

Later that night, the first snow fell. In the morning I headed down to check my vegetable patch. Everything was covered with snow now, but the empty thermoses had been returned as usual. A trail of small footprints led back and forth to the woods. I winced. The boy would have had to walk for quite a while in the open field. Easy to see, either from the sky or from a nearby truck.

I packed some more thermoses and put Chevy on a leash. It was a cold, gray day with a chill wind. As long as there wasn't more snow, the footprints would be easy to see. Chevy and I followed the trail deep into my woods and crossed onto the neighbor's woodlot. The land wasn't much use for farming, but long ago it had been logged, and my neighbor still did some cutting. The property was crisscrossed with old logging roads. I was walking with my head down, following the footprints as they turned onto a logging road. I stopped dead.

There were tire tracks on the road. Sinking deep into the snow. Slithering, spinning, as they followed the path of the footprints. Was it the American? How the hell had he found the trail? My scalp prickled. My skin grew cold. Chevy growled, a low rumble in her throat.

I broke into a jog, stumbling and slipping on the uneven road. Panting for breath, I scanned the woods ahead. Nothing. The wind was picking up. Whipping the snow into eddies. I squinted.

A flash of metal caught my eye through the snow. I ran faster. Chevy was pulling at the leash. The flash of metal became a pickup truck, stuck in the middle of the road. A mid-nineties Ford F-150. It had earned its share of dents and scrapes, and its worn tires were dug deep into the snow.

It had an Alabama license plate. Faded bumper stickers all over its tailgate. *Honk if you love Jesus. God is my co-pilot.*

And a Confederate flag.

I crept toward the truck nervously. I couldn't see anyone inside, but I wasn't taking any chances with this guy. It was a big truck, decked out with a heavy-duty suspension, tinted windows and roof lights. Once I got close enough, I tried to peer through the tinted windows. It looked empty inside.

I tried the door. It was unlocked, the keys still in the ignition. This truck wasn't going anywhere. Fast-food containers and road maps covered the passenger seat, along with a guidebook to hunting in Canada. Behind the seat were a duffel bag and a pile of blankets and pillows. On the floor of the passenger side sat a battered cardboard box of toys. All old and well used. I'm no expert on toys, but I recognized Barbies and Care Bears from when I was a kid.

I flipped open the glove compartment and found a wallet and an American passport in the name of Leonard Steele. By his birth date, he was forty-eight.

I got back out of the truck. Stared around me. Listened to the quiet. Where was the guy? Ahead, two sets of footprints led up the road. One small set followed by another made by giant boots with a thick tread.

A vise gripped my gut. I climbed into the bed of the truck. It was empty except for some grimy tools and a rusty storage box.

I opened it. It was crammed with tools and emergency equipment, but the only thing that mattered to me was the rifle case sitting on top. It was open. And empty.

Just as I was figuring out what that meant, a gunshot cracked the air.

Sixteen

The shot was still echoing when I heard a scream. Long, drawn-out and full of rage. My heart stopped. I froze, searching the woods. Where had the scream come from? Up ahead? From the side? The wind muffled sound, and the echo seemed to come from everywhere.

Chevy stood stock-still, her ears pricked. She was staring up the road. Follow the prints, I thought. I jumped down from the truck and hit the trail running. Stumbling and sliding, I raced along the road. Chevy strained on the leash, frantic to go faster.

I panted to keep up. No time to think what I would do alone against a man with a gun.

A bend appeared in the road. Between gasps for air, I heard voices. I skidded to a stop, yanking hard on Chevy's leash. I needed a plan. I couldn't charge into the middle of danger. I had to see what I was facing. And I had to make sure Chevy didn't bark. Or try to play hero.

I ducked off the road behind some cedars and tied her to a strong tree. After a whispered *Hush*, I left her. I crouched low. Started to scramble forward through the woods. The voices continued, jumbling over each other. Rough, urgent and angry. I couldn't see anything, but suddenly Robin screamed. Slicing the cold air like a knife.

"Nicky, shoot him! Shoot him!"

A man's voice replied, too soft and low to understand. Then more yelling. A large boulder loomed ahead, blocking my view.

I raced toward it, keeping low and out of sight. Pressed myself against it.

"Nicky," the man was saying, "don't you remember?"

I peered over the top of the boulder. There was a small clearing in the brush, with a lean-to made of boards and branches. A man in a camouflage vest and baseball cap was standing at the edge of the clearing. His rifle hung loosely in one hand, pointing at the ground. His gaze was fixed on Marian.

Marian was about fifteen feet away, standing just outside the lean-to. She had my mother's shotgun pointed straight at the man's chest. It weighed at least ten pounds, and she was weaker than a newborn. The shotgun trembled in her grip. But her gaze was as steady as a coyote staring down its prey.

I was roughly between them. If I stepped out, I would be right in the path of any bullets that flew from either side.

I didn't like my odds. Robin picked up a handful of snow and threw it at the man. Then a rock. An empty cup. The man didn't even duck as it hit him in the head. But his eyes turned as hard as steel.

"Shoot him!" Robin yelled. "He killed our father!"

Steele held out his free hand. I saw now it had a doll in it. "Nicky, I'm your uncle Lenny. Don't you remember? Your mama's brother? Remember I give you this doll for your eighth birthday? You had a party in the yard, barbecued wings and corn? You loved this doll. Called her Lily Mae."

For an instant, the shotgun shifted on Marian's shoulder. She blinked. Then she tightened her grip and stared down the sight.

Steele waved the doll. "Look at it! I kept it for you all these years. Never gave up—"

"Lie!" Robin grabbed a stick and rushed toward Steele. The man raised his gun. That was enough for me. I stepped out.

"Robin," I said. As quiet and calm as I could. Inside, my heart was hammering. "Don't."

Steele whirled toward me. "Who the hell are you!"

"This is my land."

"Back off. Nothing to do with you. I just come for these children."

"These children are—"

"Put the gun down!" Marian's voice was like a whip. We all spun around to look at her. She had taken half a dozen steps forward. Struggled to keep the gun propped against her shoulder. "Put. The. Gun. Down."

I was afraid she'd drop it. Or, worse, fire it. The recoil would knock her into the next county. "Marian, give me the gun."

Robin stamped his feet. "He kill our father!"

"I know, Robin. The police know." Not quite true, but I had to think fast. "They are on their way. Marian, let me handle him."

I've never been much of a hero, but I'd watched enough John Wayne movies with my mother to know how they act. How they talk. I put as much John Wayne as I could into my voice. "I can handle it."

The shotgun was already drooping. Marian lowered her eyes. They were filled with tears now as she handed me the gun. The cold steel barrel had just touched my hand when Steele made his move. He lunged at Robin, yanked him toward him and angled the rifle barrel against the boy's head.

"Now it's your turn. You put down that gun!"

Marian shrieked. I had to grab her to stop her running straight at Steele. Her eyes burned with hate.

I thought fast. "You don't want to make things worse, Lenny. These kids have been through hell, and if you care about them—"

He snorted. "I don't care about the Croat's little bastard. He's nothing but a wild animal—already tried to shoot me once. I'll shoot him if I have to. But her…" He jerked his head toward Marian. "She's coming with me. And if she wants to save her bastard son's life…"

He started to drag Robin backward toward the road. The rifle was still jammed against the boy's head. I could see the whites of Robin's eyes. But there was fury in them as well as fear. He was not going down without a fight.

Marian was trying to yank the shotgun from my grip. I hung onto her and the shotgun as best I could. But this left no free hand for me to work with. All I had were words. Not my strongest suit.

"Lenny," I said, "I know something bad happened in the past. I get that. But this will only make it worse. Do you want to end up in jail—"

"You think I'm an idiot? I'm already going to jail. This is my only shot."

"It won't work." I took a small step. "The police—"

"Back off!" Steele shouted. He jerked the rifle barrel from Robin to me. "You looking for a bullet in the head too?"

Marian had grown very still. She squeezed my arm. Hissed something in my ear. At that moment I noticed a flash of metal about six feet from Steele's big boot. The jagged edge of a trap, half buried in the snow. I peered closer. My old bear trap! I glanced around. Saw a line of smaller indents in the snow. More traps. The kids had tried to protect themselves the only way they knew.

I started circling toward the bear trap. I pulled Marian with me, hoping Steele would follow. She didn't resist. She leaned against me, weak and limp. Robin played his part too, stumbling sideways in the snow. Steele cursed and lurched.

Four feet.

Steele's boot slipped. He shifted his grip. Clamped the boy tightly for balance. Robin met my gaze. Too excited to be scared.

Two feet.

"Snow is a funny thing, Lenny—" I started. And Robin dived. Out from under Steele's arm, rolling over and over in the snow. Steele roared with surprise and leaped to grab him.

Planted his big boot right in the middle of the trap.

My bear trap was built to snap shut when more than 150 pounds hit the center plate. Leonard Steele easily fit the bill. The jaws snapped shut over his foot, biting deep into his ankle. He howled. The rifle sailed through the air and landed in the snow. Robin grabbed it. I think he would have killed the guy on the spot if I hadn't stopped him. He screamed and kicked and cried as my arms pinned him.

The angriest boy I'd ever seen.

Seventeen

It was a long hike back to my house through the snow and cold. No one said much, not even the cops when they came to take Steele away. But bright and early the next morning, Jessica Swan's cruiser came down my lane. It was followed by an ambulance and another car that looked new and shiny. Two people climbed out of it. I knew without asking who they were.

Children's Services.

Marian had hardly said a word since yesterday. Now she closed her eyes while the paramedics strapped her onto a gurney.

Robin looked at me as Children's Services packed him into their car. His eyes were pleading, but he said nothing. I could only manage a wave.

There was a lot to sort out, Jessica said. But for now they had found a good foster home for Robin in the city while Marian was in hospital.

I wanted to fight it right then and there. But I knew you don't win against Children's Services.

I watched the two vehicles disappear down the road. "Why can't they stay here until it gets sorted out?" I asked.

Jessica gave me a sad look. "Let's go inside and make coffee."

I knew that meant she had bad news. Once the coffee was poured, she sighed.

"I don't make the rules, Rick."

"But Marian is old enough. When she's better, she'll get him back, right?" I'd lain awake half the night figuring it out.

My vegetable business was growing. It had been nice having Robin around, and I could use the extra help. There were two extra bedrooms in the back of the house. Never been used. And the local school bus already drove by my lane.

"It's complicated. The Americans are coming up to interview them. Start the process to bring them home."

"Home!" I hadn't even thought about that. The homestead was the only home Robin had ever known. "What home?"

Jessica toyed with her spoon. Added way too much sugar. "The girl is Nika Horvat. Abducted from her home in Mobile, Alabama, when she was eight years old. DNA will confirm it, but we believe the body you found is her father, Luka."

"Robin says Steele shot him. I hope you guys can prove that."

She nodded. "They did the postmortem yesterday. Found the bullet. A Nosler

Partition 150 grain. Not from a .308 like the rifle we found in the barn. From a .270 like the rifle Steele had. Ballistics is working on a match. But...Steele says he didn't shoot the girl. He says Robin fired the .308, trying to hit him."

"Robin's hardly bigger than a matchstick!"

"Hurley says that's probably why he missed and hit the girl."

"The kids said it was a hunter. An accident."

Jessica looked at me over her coffee cup. For what seemed like forever, she said nothing. "There are lots of duck hunters out, for sure. I'll pass that on to the Ossington team."

I didn't dare say more. I hoped the cops wouldn't look too hard at the story. Leonard Steele belonged in jail way more than Robin did. "Did Steele confess to killing the guy?"

"Luka Horvat?" She nodded. "Oh yeah. He's singing like a canary. The FBI down in Alabama have confirmed his story. Apparently, Luka Horvat was a refugee from Croatia back in the early 1990s. He had some pretty rough times over there—saw his parents massacred by the Serbian army. Sounds like he had post-traumatic problems. Anyway, he settled in Mobile, Alabama, and married a local girl, Leonard Steele's sister, and they had a daughter named Nika. According to Steele, the sister tried to help Luka, but he was suspicious of everyone. Freaked out over small things and by the end hardly left the house. She knew it wasn't good for Nika. She finally told Luka she was leaving him. She asked her brother to come pick her up. Instead, he found her dead of multiple stab wounds, and the little girl missing. Steele's been looking for his niece ever since."

I pictured Steele finding his sister dead. Vowing to track down her killer. Filled with hate and fear, never giving up the search. "So he killed the killer."

"Steele claims it was self-defense. Says Luka came after him with the .308."

I remembered the padlocks, the chains, the deadly traps. Luka was one desperate guy. "That's possible," I said.

But Jessica shook her head. "He was shot in the back, Rick. No matter how understanding the courts might be, that's murder."

I shivered. *God is my co-pilot*, Steele had claimed. If so, hate had knocked him way off course. Steele could have been the family the kids needed. But that hate, and a bullet in the back, had changed all that. "So if the brother's going to jail, why send the kids to strangers?"

"Her parents want them, Rick. Nika is all they have left of their daughter."

"But they won't want Robin."

She shrugged. "They said they'll try. They sound like really nice people."

Try. *Try!* What kind of welcome was that for a kid who'd known nothing but a cup, a bowl and a bedroll in a barn all his life? Who'd never been taught to read or even talk, let alone play baseball and video games.

My eyes prickled. I knew if I talked any more, I might lose it. Robin was going into a world of strangers. Big city, strange school, kids who wouldn't understand. He might as well be landing on Mars. But the worst was that whenever his new family looked at him, they would see that Croat's little bastard. Not their grandson, not a scared little boy. But a killer's son.

"It won't work," I managed to say.

She reached across the table. Her fingertips touched my hand. "We don't make the rules, Rick. But he's young. And he's a fighter."

Fighting isn't what he needs, I wanted to say. I looked at her fingers on mine. Slipped my own around them, just for an instant. Before Robin, I'd never felt alone. Never wished there was someone else.

Maybe that was the night thief's gift.

Acknowledgments

The village of Lake Madrid and Madrid County are fictional, but their resemblance to real communities is not coincidental. Lake Madrid stands for all the struggling rural farming communities whose traditions and ties run deep.

I would like to thank Andrew Wooldridge and Bob Tyrrell, publishers of the dynamic and innovative Orca Books, for continuing to believe in me and in this series, and my terrific editor, Ruth Linka, whose insightful questions and critiques made *The Night Thief* a better book. I'd also like to thank Barry Brown of Port Dover, Ontario, for his expertise in rifles, and my good friend and fellow writer Vicki Delany for her thoughtful suggestions on an earlier draft.

BARBARA FRADKIN is a child psychologist with a fascination for how we turn bad. Her compelling short stories haunt numerous magazines and anthologies, but she is best known for her gritty, psychological detective series featuring Ottawa Police Inspector Michael Green. Barbara won Arthur Ellis Best Novel Awards for both *Fifth Son* (2005) and *Honour Among Men* (2007). Barbara's work as a school psychologist helping adolescents and younger children, many of whom struggle with reading, has also made her a strong advocate of programs that help to develop reading as a lifelong passion. For more information, visit barbarafradkin.com.

Read the first two titles in the Cedric O'Toole mystery series

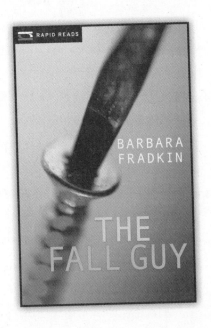

Cedric O'Toole is a reluctant and unlikely hero who lives alone on a scrub farm trying to eke out a living as a country handyman. Follow Cedric as he unwittingly finds himself in the middle of one mystery after another.

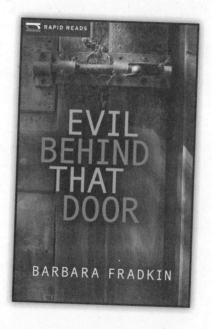

"Fradkin successfully brings back her handyman/inventor hero in his second outing (after *The Fall Guy*)...Plenty of suspense and action are packed into a short and satisfying story."
—*Library Journal*

RAPID READS
WWW.RAPID-READS.COM

DISCOVER GAIL BOWEN'S
CHARLIE D MYSTERIES

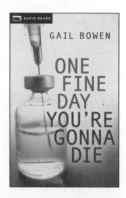

Charlie D is the host of a successful late-night radio call-in show, *The World According to Charlie D.* Each of these novels features a mystery that is played out in a race against time as Charlie D fights to save the innocent and redeem himself.

Meet the Goddaughter...

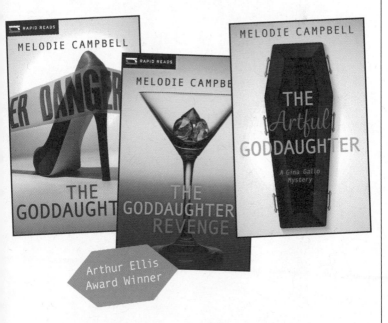

MELODIE CAMPBELL

THE GODDAUGHTER

MELODIE CAMPBELL

THE GODDAUGHTER REVENGE

Arthur Ellis Award Winner

MELODIE CAMPBELL

THE Artful GODDAUGHTER

A Gina Gallo Mystery

Gina Gallo is a gemologist who would like nothing better than to run her little jewelry shop. Unfortunately she's also the "Goddaughter." Try as she might, Gina can't escape the family business.

RAPID READS
WWW.RAPID-READS.COM